Chocolate Chip Cookies

by Karen Wagner
illustrated by Leah Palmer Preiss

Henry Holt & Company
New York

Published by Henry Holt and Company, Inc., 115 West 18th Street, New York, New York 10011.
Published in Canada by Fitzhenry & Whiteside Limited,
195 Allstate Parkway, Markham, Ontario L3R 4T8.

Library of Congress Cataloging-in-Publication Data
Wagner, Karen. Chocolate chip cookies / by Karen Wagner ; illustrated by Leah Palmer Preiss.
Summary: Twin boys follow a simple recipe for baking chocolate chip cookies.
ISBN 0-8050-1268-0   [1. Chocolate chip cookies—Fiction.   2. Baking—Fiction.]
I. Preiss, Leah Palmer, ill.   II. Title.
PZ7.W12428Ch 1990 [E]—dc20   89-39794

Henry Holt books are available at special discounts for bulk purchases for sales promotions, premiums,
fund-raising, or educational use. Special editions or book excerpts can also be created to specification.
For details contact: Special Sales Director, Henry Holt and Company, Inc.,
115 West 18th Street, New York, New York 10011

Printed in the United States of America
3   5   7   9   10   8   6   4   2

Ready

Measure

Sift

Cream

Crack

Beat

Stir

Pour

Chop

Mix

Spoon

Lick

Bake

Smell

Taste

Chocolate Chip Cookies

Preheat oven to 375°.

2¼ cups unsifted all-purpose
  flour
1 teaspoon baking soda
1 teaspoon salt
1 cup butter, softened
¾ cup granulated sugar

¾ cup firmly packed brown
  sugar
2 eggs
1 teaspoon vanilla extract
1 cup nuts (optional)
2 cups chocolate chips

Get **ready** by washing your hands. **Measure** flour, baking soda, and salt. **Sift** dry ingredients together and set aside. **Cream** butter, granulated sugar, and brown sugar in a bowl. **Crack** eggs into the bowl. **Beat** the eggs with butter mixture till smooth. **Stir** in vanilla. **Pour** dry ingredients into the bowl. **Chop** nuts (optional). **Mix** in nuts and chocolate chips. **Spoon** by the teaspoonful onto an ungreased cookie sheet. Don't forget to **lick** the spoon! **Bake** 9–11 minutes or until cookies are golden brown and **smell** delicious. Allow to cool, and **taste.**

Mmmmm!